All In A Day's Work
and Other Stories

An Anthology of work written by
Spark Young Writers
during 2020 - 2021

Co-funded by the
Creative Europe Programme
of the European Union   READ ON

COPYRIGHT

ISBN 9798546439002

Spark Young Writers is a Project of
Writing West Midlands

Edited by Emma Boniwell

With thanks to:
All the Spark Lead and Assistant Writers
The Spark Young Writers
&
The Spark Team at WWM

About Writing West Midlands

Writing West Midlands is the literature development agency for the West Midlands region of the UK. We run events and activities for writers and readers, including our annual Birmingham Literature Festival. We also run Spark Young Writers, which is a major programme of work for young writers aged 8 to 16+ including regular workshops, a summer school and a magazine. Writing West Midlands also works with libraries, publishers and universities to help creative writers develop their skills.

About READ ON!

READ ON! is a major Creative Europe funded project across six European countries working in five languages. It aims to encourage young people aged 12 to 19 to engage with reading and creative writing. Writing West Midlands is the UK partner. This Anthology has been produced as part of this project.

Spark Anthology 2021

For the first time, Spark Young Writers have made an anthology of work they have produced during the year.

Our groups have been forced to take place online, which has been difficult for some of our young writers. We haven't been able to hold our annual Awards Ceremony which is usually one of the highlights of the Writing West Midlands year.

So we have asked all our young writers – even those who only managed one or two sessions with us – if they would like to contribute a short piece for our Anthology.

We have a varied collection of poems, stories, scripts, letters and reviews. Some have been written collectively, most independently.

Our young writers range from 7 – 17 years old.

Special thanks must be given to our incredible team of lead and assistant writers, who learnt new skills and adapted their working practises to work online and deliver nearly 200 workshops in this year of COVID restrictions:

Romalyn Ante, Sara-Jane Arbury, Jean Atkin, George Bastow, Charley Barnes, Ian Billings, Jen Burrows, Helen Calcutt, Olivia Chalmers, Elisabeth Charis, Nellie Cole, Sylvia Crawley, Ben Davis, Greg Dimmock, Emily Edge, William Gallagher, Cindy George, Fiona Harding, Aisha Iftikhar, Catrin Jackson, Lauren James, Emilie Lauren Jones, Aidan Kavanagh, Dawn Lewis, Aoife Mannix, Patrick McConnell, Kibriya Mehrban, Lou Minns, Dan Mountain, Hikmah Muhammed, Sara Myers, Amarjit Nar, Ken Preston, Emma Purshouse, Stephanie Ridings, Mandy Ross, Jordan Sam Adams, Rick Sanders, Mary Skertchley, Ruth Stacey, Susan Stokes-Chapman, Christine Strathie, Scarlett Ward-Bennett, Maria Whatton, Laura Whetton, Martin Yates.

With thanks to our funders Arts Council England and Creative Europe

Spark Young Writers groups 2020-2021

Bartley Green	(school years 3-6)
Birmingham 1	(school years 3-6)
Birmingham 2	(school years 7-13)
Birmingham 3	(school years 5-8)
Coventry	(school years 3-6)
Edgbaston	(school years 7-13)
Kidderminster	(school years 7-13)
Leamington	(school years 7-13)
Ledbury	(school years 5-9)
Online Junior	(school years 3-6)
Online Teen	(school years 7-13)
Rugby	(school years 5-8)
Shrewsbury	(school years 3-6)
Stoke upon Trent	(school years 5-9)
Stratford	(school years 7–13)
Tamworth	(school years 6-9)
Telford	(school years 3-6)
Wolverhampton	(school years 7-13)
Worcester	(school years 5-8)

Table of Contents

Poems

Prose

Miscellaneous

Collective writing

Some of our groups decided to write pieces together

Spark Torch
by Ealingee, Jonathan, Joseph and Samarah,
with Aisha and Mandy
Collective writing by Zoom Chat

Birmingham 1

Spark! A small flame, particle of fire,
explosion of colours, star shedding light in the dark
sky.
Spark! A funny feeling, idea glittering.
It pops, buzzes, fizzes, bursts into happiness.

This Spark began with brand new notebooks, pencils
and pens,
tablet, computer or phone, and our brains.
We felt happy-nervous-excited, tingly fingertips,
butterflies in tummies,
looking-forward-to-it-not-sure-if-we-wanted-to.

Writing starts with a capital letter, a fronted adverbial,
an expanded noun phrase,
or an idea, a picture, once upon a time...
a thought, something to share,
words in our heads that we want to write down.

On the screen together we're stressed or calm, happy, excited.
We're writers writing, thinking, imagining,
wishing we could be good at everything,
wish we could do this every day.

We've shared story ideas, thoughts, tips and laughs,
riddles and rhymes, haiku and crazy stories.
This Spark ends with enjoyment, fun, creativity, a game
and feelings, sad feelings, which are at the same time happy.

We'll carry this spark onwards like a torch. A torch of writing!
One idea leads to another as a match lights a sparkler,
as one sparkler gives life to another.
Light a firework, light an invitation, light a spark.
Keep writing!

June 2021

This Glass of Water
by Ealingee, Jonathan, Joseph and Samarah,
with Aisha and Mandy
Collective writing by Zoom Chat

This glass of water feels liquid, smooth, cool, fresh.
It tastes of nothing, like air, transparent, clean, cold,
refreshing.
It smells of ice, of outside, of silence!
It sounds like the sea as it glugs.
Shhh… It is still. It sounds of nothing.

It looks like a mirror. The light at the top ripples,
reflects.
When I type these words it makes the water jiggle just
a little.
When I go to drink… it swishes.
Imagine drinking the light, lighting my tummy.

How old is the water?
Not old. I poured it from the tap, from the pipe.
Ten minutes old, maybe half of an hour.
Where did it come from?
It fell from the air, from the clouds as rain,
clouds over the sea, water vapour,
or rain in the river which flowed into the sea.
How old? Five hours? A few days? As old as the Earth itself?
It's fresh water but ancient, four billion years old?
Makes me feel I've gone back in time...

Water in the lake, the river, streams,
in the sink, the sea, the bath, the swimming pool,
in puddles, in clouds, the ocean, the pond in the park,
a leak in the roof, in rain, hail, snow, ice,
and the water in my glass
has been as deep as an ocean,
as blue as a lake, as annoying as a leak,
as shallow as a sink, as black as night sea,
as clear as ice, as hard as hail,
as soft as snow, as calm as water in a cup,
as drenching as the waves, as fierce as a tsunami,
as still and shallow, as deep, splashy, muddy as a puddle,

as warm and relaxing as a bath
as refreshing as a splash of water on your face
as welcome as when you're thirsty after tennis or
football or hockey.
Sip.
Slurp
Gulp.
Glug.
Swallow.
I wish I could drink a glass of rain.

June 2021

Words
By Rugby Spark Group

Little black seeds on the big barren page,
animal sleeping.

Which words will win when wanting to write?
Planted in minds growing stage by stage.

Page envy.

Woman was afraid of going on stage –
from stage pink to free reading –
atomic literature.

Letters make no difference as lone raindrops.

      Sesquipedalian.

But as a downpour of words, they nurture growth,
ice falling from caves,
creepy shadows lurk behind.

Literature's atoms, the building blocks of books.
Owned by no one used by all.

Yellow sun beams,
tricky to work with.

Background music to life.

Poems

These poems were written during or inspired by Spark
Young Writers group sessions.

FLASH!
By Oliver Bryant

Online Junior

Once the time had gone, all hopes would be trashed.
All I had done, game set and match.
The ball was stolen by some imbecile,
Probably now buying bone meal.

FLASH!

3 more chances to go,
Where is the ball? Oh, no no no!
I left it near a swamp on Marylebone Road,
In which case it may have been stolen by a toad?!
The ball should flash in less than a minute,
I hear the birds saying 'Twit twit'.

FLASH!

Something is wrong, it's been at least a minute,
By now I really am feeling rather miffed.
Oh no, my last hope is here -
Then I see a gleam quite near.

DONE IT! Finally found my ball,
Actually, not mine but Paul's.
Really shouldn't have reacted like the end of the world.

From Night to Morning
By Mark Chappell

Driving in the dark.
The wind roaring through my hair.
Headlights dazzling a deer on its midnight walk.
As tinny Britpop blares into the fields.

A nocturnal sheep staring at me,
As if asking why I'm disturbing it at this unholy hour.
The cows don't seem to care though.
The bovine ear is obviously much more appreciative
of Oasis.

Fresh grassy smells materialise as dawn breaks
And the first sweet drops of dew congregate
On my windscreen.
Morning has broken.

Ode to a Radiator
By Maeve Deegan

Telford

Oh, how I love your clean white figure,
That heats me on cold nights,
And is turnable-offable via a dial.
You are my favourite thing connected to the boiler,
and your very presence is warming to my soul,
And though spiders build their cobwebs where you are
connected to the wall,
I could not think of a better rectangle to heat my room
on the coldest of days,
and to turn off so obediently when I ask you to.
Oh, I cannot love you any more, radiator.

A Monster is Born
By Arav Desi

Stratford

The dark shadows looming,
Across the night façade of London,
The thugs roar with unruly harmony,
But as they release terror up into the smoky skies,
As blood-shot wolves,
Roam the deserted streets,
A forsaken child roams.

He comes upon the pebbled cold streets,
Glaring coldly from below,
The walls whisper in the chilling air,
They speculate the fate of the child,
Forgotten in the fog of the city.
And as he roams across looking for a way to beauty of
the light,
The thunderous spies of the night stalk him.

He approaches the swine of the dark,
The timid fool scutters to the alleyways,
Where only fear can strike,
The crowds of demons riot against the good,
Peckish for revenge,
Against their tangled past,
The hunting begins.

The insect speeds across the witches and mutants,
Looking for an escape from the reality of this
nightmare,
The claws of robbery take their grip,
Upon his frail arms,
And he with his feeble-minded brain,
Begs for mercy to the faceless terror,
His words of hope echo into the void.
The beasts now feast upon their prey,
Stripping the naïve child,
Exposing him with the harshness of the cold-blooded
kind,
His weeps of innocence turn into bellows of hate,
The years pass on to this kidnapped little child,
The wickedness of the underworld groom him,
A monster is born.

Lost Souls
By Ella Goldberg

Edgbaston

Two lost souls
Were they once one?
Connected by body, mind, emotions
Entwined in love
But now broken.
Looking for the place
They both belong -
in each other's arms.

Some will go to great lengths
To find the one:
Making mistakes,
Leaving a trail
Of friendship,
love and heartbreak.
Yet always believing it'll be worth it
in the end.

 But how do they know if they've met the one?
And what if they don't want someone?
is this what we call love?

Ode to a Vampire Bat
By Emily Lonsdale

Birmingham 2

Desmodus Rotundus named simply
For body, your slim form
And fine brown hairs, like a distinguished gentleman
Thin and fading to grey.

Your song is silent,
But your movement speaks volumes
A thousand ghost stories in the clatter of flight
The one mammal that can fly yet only at night.

Your wings so delicate, bones touching skin
You duck and you weave, you twirl and you swirl
A matador's cape, yet only so thin

Your ears could be cute on another beast
Huge and clumsy, feathery, and pink
Like an exotic wine we never want to drink

Your snout is a wonder even covered in blood, hiding
twenty-two perfect teeth
Only half of them in use. It draws up round those inky
black voids, sneers
As you lap the blood with your tiny red tongue

You have carved the perfect niche, you have made a
chilling story
Fly through the nightmares, with half your body
weight in blood
And an infinite mythological glory.

The Moon
By Hannah Lumb

Ledbury

The moon
The simplest way to start a story
There are many tales about it
None like this one
This one is unique
Close your eyes
Now you are speeding through an iridescent forest
Shimmering at night
Past the derelict settlement
Past the living
Past the dead
Stop
There is a girl in the clearing here
Can you see her?
Her name is Hexyl
She has been here for centuries
Never has she moved from her clearing
Hexyl's clearing
A cursed clearing
Where the moon shines bright for all to see
The moon
Pale, celestial, mesmerising
Majestic, magical

Stardust white
Don't be deceived by Hexyl's moon
She stares
The moon's bright eye
Hexyl stares, eyes burning
In love with the moon
She always will be
Always will
Always will
She cannot stop
Cannot stop
Cannot stop
Her blank stone eyes
Locked to her blank stone mind
Waiting
Waiting
Waiting, for someone to finish her story

Eulogising Aspen
By Maisy Mansell-Warren

Wolverhampton

The way she looked through those binoculars
you'd think she was spying on angels.
I'll never tire of the memory of her
bare feet in the brook,
the speckled sunlight pouring through the
trees, from the water and onto her face.

She broke through air, through silence,
through everything in fact.
Through me.
Love
is a pitiful word
when all I feel is the copper glint
in her squinted eyes as she watched
the insects in the grass.

The horse chestnut she lay under all those
hours,
with her jars and coded letters and
picked wildflowers
is dying
of a broken heart without her
friendship.

I lie beneath it now
and it drops its decaying flowers on my
chest where my heart used to beat.
There's no reason why it should beat now.
The flowers are offerings,
I suppose,
sacrifices
because move over Achlys,
your feeble mists mean
nothing to the gaping hole in my life
that only she can fill.

Immigrant story
By Krishan Nayyar

Online Junior

Step into the new land
Let your wishes come true
Work like a dog
And be grateful

Brother parted from brother
Sister torn from sister
New lives only get told stories of their grandmother
And a land they will never call home

Work harder
Earn more
Educate the next generation
And things will get better

Equality beckons
Grades not based on colour
Hard work shines
And graduation pictures are on the wall

Reality hits
It's all a lie
This land isn't ours
And neither is the one left behind

Stand up and protest
Let your voice be heard
Take the knee
And let them tell you there's no issue

Now where do we belong
Where our colour comes from or this new home
Immigrant forever
And yet we're the problem

Vaquita
By Evelyn Noonan

Coventry

I fly and I glide
I whizz through the waves
I feel the water and its warm embrace.
Like a vanquished web I am more than free
Whilst the blue still surrounds me.
I sail and I spree but as more surrounds me
No, it's not blue,
Then more than scary
It's black and white, too
As I slide through the sea
My sail is cut off
As I soar through the ocean
I'm suddenly strapped
Is this the end?
May I no longer fly?
I can't take a final breath
I wait for the pain.

But then
this time

like a felled web I'm free again
Whilst the blue surrounds me
I sail and spree
I glide through the blue
I reach for the coral
The sea is then humble

I'm happy I live
For few of us do
And, if only for your voice,
I'm glad that you do, too.

This Window
By Felami Ogunmiluyi

Online Teen

The sky feels dead,
It has no colour.
This window of mine makes me see the world in a
different light,
But I know that it can't be changed.
This window of mine likes to change my view,
However, it can't do that to you.

This window of mine seems a bit dirty,
But I won't know that until I'm thirty.
This window of mine is going to be cleaned,
It was almost like we were meant to be teamed.

This window of mine now seems happy,
I now know why it was so trashy.

Kindness
By Chloe Pick

Online Teen

Kindness is a red autumnal tree
Who sits all alone
In an echoing valley
Who waits for a friend
When winter comes,
The snow falls
And a show is put on
Just for the lonely tree

Hope
By Chloe Pick

Online Teen

Swirling in the depths of my mind,
Doubt rules supreme
Quashing the rebellion of hope
I can't find a way out of the storm
There is no shelter as waves of hopelessness batter me
Every thought dictated, every memory tarnished
I don't know how this started
All I know is that I need to end it

Darkness engulfs me for months on end
Then the doubt weakens
Just for a second
But that was all that I needed
A beacon of light finally breaks through the dark
clouds
Illuminating the forest of imagination
As animals fill my mind with endless possibilities
A rainforest coming to life in an instant
Spotlighting vast oceans of knowledge
Where schools of fish discuss the storm
And restoring years of knowledge
Igniting my happiness into a roaring fire that will
never die out
And rekindling my love of life
Because now I know that no storm lasts forever

Pencil Tip
By Fanni Doroti Polgar

Online Teen

I stand on the edge of a pencil tip -
my mind in conflict,
should I slip?
Is this the life I want to live?
How much of myself am I right to give?

I can only ever write what I truly believe,
it is not within my nature to deceive.
But who am I to throw my soul away when I often
struggle to understand myself?
In the deep end of emotion – the love. The losses.
My greatest devotion…

I stand on the edge of a pencil tip -
my hands are shaking whilst my soul is waking
Who am I if I do not allow myself to slip?
This is the life I have chosen to live,
this is the part of myself I have chosen to give...

Gratitude
By Fanni Doroti Polgar

Online Teen

There is a place I know where no wave can wash away
the smile;
there is a place I know where songs of serendipity
silence all sounds of sorrow.
There is a place I know which can be right where you
are yet further than the furthest mile;
there is a place I know where the present is key, and
nobody fears the events of tomorrow.

There is a place,
luminous, colourful, wonderful.
There is a place,
jovial, appreciated, powerful.

There is a place by the name of Gratitude:
a place I know that welcomes without condition.
My mother once told me that finding yourself sat at its
centre is determined by your attitude.
Gratitude is the state of feeling grateful, by definition.

Be at war with none,
and with peace always be at one.

Mirror Poem
By Ealingee Rajeevan

Birmingham 1

I am a mirror,
I am shiny and bright,
But when the light,
Isn't so bright,
I cannot see,
The plain white wall.
It is plain,
But…
As I have seen it for so long,
It seems…
I have gotten attached to it.
When someone looks in me,
I feel unhappy because…
I am trying to look at…
The plain white wall.

The Mystery Hand...
By Avani Singh

Online Junior

The fire crackled,
I added more log.
Something was cackling,
But all I could see was fog.

The flames spitted,
I heard some sort of metal burn.
Something was ill fitted,
Whatever was wrong, I had to learn.

The smoke rised,
A fresh aroma filled the room.
Something was disguised.
Was it pleasant or was it doom?

What reached out next was a hand,
It was dirty and mucky.
Where was it to land?
It seemed that if I survived, I was lucky.

The gnarled fingers of the hand curled around,
It was a surprisingly petrifying scare.
Other than my heart beat there was no sound,
If I could make a wish, it would be that this is a
nightmare.

Lighthouse
By Liang Zi

Junior online

I was looking out with my shining light,
Trying to find the extremely rare sight.
Legend has it that if you're in a lighthouse,
You might see this glowing mouse.

I shone my light to my West,
And looked for this mystic pest.
They say that this little mouse,
Steals from a sea house.

No, no mouse here,
No mouse that I can see.
No mouse skipping here and there,
No mouse skipping on the sea.

To my East I shine my light,
But still, I cannot see the sight.
People say that the mouse can sense,
When people are really tense.

No, no mouse here,
No mouse that I can see.
No mouse skipping here and there,
No mouse skipping on the sea.

Over there to my South,
I see the mouse's mouth.
Hooray, Hooray I saw its bells,
Oh no it's gone somewhere else.

The mouse carries ding dong bells,
To substitute its tiny yells.
I saw it, I saw it but I need some proof,
That I saw it whilst under this roof.

Over to the North I look,
No mouse carrying a heavy book.
0Why, OH WHY did I not watch it go,
For I don't see it now, just letting you know.

Prose

These pieces were written during or inspired by Spark
Young Writers group sessions.

Getting lost at M & S
By Finlay Ager

Coventry

It was Sunday, which is shopping day. This time we were going to M&S. When we were there, I saw a cool t-shirt I wanted to buy. I went and grabbed it, but when I turned back my mum wasn't there. I looked and looked but couldn't find her. I went to the counter, but she wasn't there. In the next three hours, I was starting to get bored when all of a sudden, I heard my mother. When I saw her, I showed her the t-shirt, but when we took it to the counter, the person said it was £150. My mum fainted.

The End.

Last One Left
By Uma Ahluwalia

Ledbury

I wake up aching all over and lazily open one eye. I blink once, then twice. Is that... the sky? Or the sea? Whatever it is, it's very blue and very glittery. I reach for my phone and instead feel something slippery and wet - it's a fish.

"AAAARGH. If this is another one of your stupid pranks, Trixie, I will rip your head off and put it on a stick in my room," I growl. I listen a second, but there is no response.

"Trixie?" Trixie is my younger sister. We have to share a room. It's really unfair - I'm five years older and so much more responsible and yet Kevin gets to have his own room instead of me.

I open my eyes fully and all I can see is water surrounding me. And I'm in a boat. In the middle of nowhere. This seems too much of an elaborate prank even for Trixie. I decide to wait a while for her to come bursting into the room and explain how she pulled off her latest mastermind prank, and I can ruffle her hair and tell her she nearly got me this time.

After waiting for what seemed like hours but must only have been a matter of minutes, I decide that Trixie isn't coming. And nor is anyone else. I'm going to have to sort this mess out on my own. I would write more, but I think I'm going to have to start rationing resources now.

Five Students VS The End Of The World
By Naomi Allen

I had five room-mates, and we were all crammed into small student accommodation next to the main road of a heavily polluted town.

We sucked.

I was short and grubby, and owned two pairs of jeans that belonged to my mum in the 80s and a woollen jumper that unravelled a tiny bit more every time I put it on.

James was rich but claimed he wanted to live amongst the "common folks"; as you can guess, he was the snobbiest of all snobs.

Amma owned two cats, and James was allergic.

Andrei dreamed of being a famous writer, and because he was pretentious he chose to write everything using a typewriter.

And my fifth room-mate? They didn't turn up until the Kraken ascended.

The world had been thrown into chaos and it was only 7:18 in the morning. My astrobiology professor had sent my class a link on how to make a tin foil hat.

People were raiding Poundland.

The CIA had been called in.

The FBI had been called in.

The Russian Foreign Intelligence Service had been called in.

Across the world, armies and special forces were buckling up to take the prophesied monster down.

And at the door to our flat, a leather jacket-wearing person with a mullet showed up. They were chewing gum, popped it and spat it at my feet.

"Hey," they looked at me distastefully. "You lot have to kill the Kraken."

I hadn't even had my morning coffee yet.

My Life in Colour
By Amelia Arnold

Tamworth

When I was 2, I saw in colour for the first time. There was an amazing red truck - yet my world was still covered in darkness.

When I was 12, I saw the most vibrant shade of blue as a patch of sky lit up and the relaxing shade flooded my vision - but still, my world was in black and white.

When I was 22, I met you, and suddenly my world lit up. I smiled and took it all in; your flushed cheeks, honey eyes and the most loving smile. You were my yellow and I grasped onto that colour with my life.

When I was 32, I was taken, and I saw black and white once more. The jumpsuit was itchy and uncomfortable, but I held on to the patch of blue sky through the cell bars. I guess that's what I deserved for being a girl in love with another girl.

I never got to 42.

The Daffodil Field
By Amelie Baker

Edgbaston

I gaze at our house from the garden, not wanting to know if my dad needs help with my mom's funeral. All I can see is her sometimes, lying peaceful and pale on the tiled floor. I hate it, thinking of her in that way instead of the warm, bubbly person she used to be.

Turning away from the house, I spin to the beat in my head — mom loved to dance. The trees are motionless, until a gush of sickening sweet air makes the leaves move. Little pockets of sunshine seep through the canopy of leaves, creating dapples of gold; she would love to see this, I close my eyes.

As they flutter back open, the black of my funeral dress swirls around me and I am once again taken over by despair. As tears trickle down my cheeks, I blink up at the crisp clean blue sky — away from the harsh empty black.

"It's time to go!" dad shouts from the house.

Dawdling solemnly to the car, I realise it's time to say goodbye. Watching from the backseat window, I make no attempt to speak as we head off.

A fluorescent yellow field of daffodils passes —
mom's favourite. One flower lies battered; hanging
limply from the stem. "Dad, stop the car!" I shout.
Before the car has had chance to stop, I have slammed
the door shut — I flee towards my field of life and
death.

Selkies Hate Toes
By Bridey Bingley

Leamington

The sand is hot and dry between my toes. Toes are weird. I'm not sure whether I'll miss them or not. I think I'll miss fingers though. Lot more useful than toes. I edge towards the wave slowly creeping up the beach. The water is cold, colder than I remember. I have to be fully submerged, though, before I can transform.

I've always found swimming as a human weird. I'm never quite sure what I'm meant to be doing with my limbs, so they just flail around a little.

I'm quite far out now. I think I'll just start. I'm tired of being a human, of having things these weird things like toes that don't even do anything. So, I dive down, deep below the surface of the water. The water starts to sting so I close my eyes.

It starts with my feet, as always. The skin re-grows, the bones and tissues and ligaments shifting and stretching to accommodate the new skin - all shiny and slippery. And toeless. The change shreds through me. The water is soothing against the ache that always accompanies re-growing skin. It's easier to shed - to become human. I would have probably stayed a human if not for toes. And those weird blobby bits on the outside of the head. Ears, I think (why ears need to stick out like that is beyond me).

I open my eyes and the darkness parts. Questionable bits of algae float amongst the murky depths. I'm home.

Everyday Hero
By Zoë Chapman

Bartley Green

This morning I woke up and felt like an extraordinary person. Someone who could do anything.

So I went outside, and held my hand out and just like magic the wind stopped blowing and the clouds parted and the sun shone as bright as bright can be.

I walked to the nearest hospital, held out my hands and every single person instantly forgot why they were there.

I had ended Coronavirus!

The Devil You Know
By Lilli Davies

Tamworth

I remember the gentle breeze through the mottled Autumn leaves, possibly even more vividly than the blood. I had marked it the second I got out of the car: bright flashes of orange and yellow and red, trying their hardest to devour the last few hopeful patches of green. All of them were swaying softly, almost awkwardly, as if they were reluctant guests at a party. Perfection.

Until he screamed.

That godforsaken scream cleaved through the tranquillity with so much force that I flinched. Turning away from that heavenly view, I fixed my gaze on his face. Wide, fearful eyes. Tousled brown hair. Blood smearing his right cheek, just a little to the left of his nose.

Maybe I was wrong. Maybe this was perfection.

Theo cringed as Henry's expression morphed – from thoughtful to a burning rage, then to a sincere smile right at him. He knew what that meant, knew because he had seen that same look just half an hour ago. Crying out was never his intention, but when Henry had pulled that axe from the truck bed...

The full weight of the situation hit him then. Zac was dead, and he knew too much. So here he was frightened and alone, in the middle of nowhere, and about to die at the hands of his best friend. Paralysed with fear, he watched a bead of crimson blood slide from the blade. Before it hit the ground, Henry lunged forward, the grin still fixed upon his lips.

King Birdeous
By Maeve Deegan

Telford

The glowing fire warmed King Birdeous's enchanting palace. Outside, the icy wind drove ruthlessly across the external walls, threatening to whisk any bird flying outside away over the treetops.

The king's servants were glad of their job, as the huge inferno presented warmth not only to the cold, rich tapestries that lined the walls, but everything inside those cosy walls. The fire crackled freely in the grate, and King Birdeous ate ravenously from a colossal platter of food.

The amount of food he was served could have fed all of the bird nests in the kingdom, including many more from beyond his empire on that isolated winter's night. Another advantage for the bird servants was that, although they had to cook the food, they consumed the leftovers themselves, and they were safe and well fed inside the palace walls.

All of the other birds would endure a brutal winter, whereas they, along with King Birdeous, would be happy and without concern.

The Assassin's Chase
By Orla Dunphy

Worcester

Standing in a corner, she watched the prince as he danced amidst the suits and ballgowns. He was her target for the night. She could feel the dagger hidden in the bodice of her golden dress. It wasn't easy to kill a prince at his own party, especially with such a small weapon. At least not for a normal person. But she wasn't a normal person, she was the world's top assassin. She downed her champagne and looked back to the prince. He was gone.

She got to the hallway and started running. Then she heard footsteps. It was a good thing she was trained for this. She slipped off her shoes and crept along the floor. She saw the prince running up the staircase and out onto the balcony. Tossing aside her heels, she sprinted behind him, launching into a full-scale chase. He ran through the French windows onto the balcony, windows slamming shut behind him.

Carefully, so as not to draw attention to herself, she opened the window, dagger in hand. Before she could move, she was pinned to the wall, her dagger in the prince's hand. He looked in her eyes and whispered, "Was that meant for me, darling?"

One Night
By Anna F

Coventry

The sky looked as though it was on fire. It was a flaming red mess of deep ambers and rich ochre. The bloodshot moon shone an eerie red light across the open savannah. A gunshot sounded. It echoed across the planes like a storm cloud in a land of sunlight. The rhino collapsed. Wheezing it lay vulnerable on the baked earth like an open wound. The predators edged closer. Creeping like panthers in for the kill. The last thing that rhino heard was the sound of ominous victory whoops and cheers. They had won this battle.

The sky looked as though it was heavy with the weight of pessimism. It was a mash of dreary, pigeon greys and dull relentless blues. She couldn't sleep. Not with what was going on in Zimbabwe and Kenya. Her tired, grey eyes wanted to close but they wouldn't.

Her head was alive with frustrated energy. 'How can they do this! How can they kill an animal for its horn? A horn that is made out of the same stuff as our fingernails and hair?' she fumed. 'The horn is only magical on the animal' she argued to herself. 'Daily now they slaughter innocent animals for their supposedly supernatural features. What did they ever do to us?' She rose from her bed and walked towards the window. She knew right now a precious life had been ended.

The Sound Of Time
By Nicholas Forbes Saunders

Online Junior

The wrinkled old fingers of the man gently caressed the keys of the piano.

He played fast with *staccato* as he revisited the hallways he walked through as a child. After a few moments the melody shifted to legato and he was back again holding hands in the moonlight with his first love.

Then there was a sudden *crescendo* as he saw the birth of his child, young and fragile like porcelain. He watched as that porcelain was forged into iron-willed stubbornness and how that stubbornness protected his child through adult life.

Later came the sudden *affannato* of loss as his beloved died. For years after there was a constant hatred that he held for the world.

Eventually, time healed those wounds leaving only the endless blur and monotony of old age. This was interrupted only by the grandchildren visiting. They gave him a light within the darkness and the *diminuendo* of memories.

Soon he forgot things.

His own child.

Soon he saw things.

He saw ghosts of old friends and lovers alike.

Soon the memories came only when he played.

So he did.

Every waking minute he could, he spent playing his old piano; even if he was judged by all those around him he played without care. He refused to leave it because he knew that the second that he did that he would lose himself again.

Tears rolled down his face as the wrinkled old fingers of the man gently caressed the keys of the piano.

Fresh Hunt
By Kevin Ge

Bartley Green

The lush green grass tickled his paws as Dusty padded across the garden. Having already eaten his daily meal of plain, dry biscuits he longed for a wilder life. The easy, comfortable life of a pet cat just didn't seem to fit him. As if by magic, a grey dot suddenly popped up on the flowerbed. Licking his lips, Dusty stealthily prowled up to it, tensing his muscles, ready to pounce… "Hey, what's up Dusty?" meowed Blaze, Dusty's neighbour and best friend. The mouse had vanished into Snowball's patch.

"Blaze! I was gonna kill the mouse, but then you interrupted me! Come on! It went to Snowball's garden!" mewed Dusty. Blaze's fiery red and orange fur turned gold under the sunlight. Both cats darted through the hedge. "Snowball!" Dusty called. Instantly a pure white cat leapt from behind Dusty.

"The mouse came into mine, but I don't -" Snowball stammered, her soft white fur standing out against the vivid green.

"I see it, over there!" Blaze meowed and pointed his paw at a nearby hedge. Snowball prowled without a sound towards the hedge as if she was a ninja. Gracefully, she pounced. Yet Dusty saw the grey dot dart towards a plum tree bearing sweet juicy fruits. Immediately, Dusty sprang forward, and in one quick swipe, killed the mouse.

"I did it!" He exclaimed, overflowing with pride. This was his first kill! He bit into the soft, tender flesh and found it exhilarating. His first kill!

Untitled
By Ella Heath-Kime

Stratford

Picture a girl, running down a shadowy, deserted street. The colours are too bright; the world looks unreal. Images crystallise and blur, kaleidoscopic, through her watery eyes. Her ragged clothes fly behind her as she skids, collapsing before a pool of red and a small body, bent at unnatural angles.

Around the two, everything disintegrates into colours and lights, the figures frozen in time for a second, an eternity. A harsh, guttural sob escapes the kneeling figure, as the lying girl shakily, unsteadily, reaches out and guides the other's head down so their foreheads touch.

Tear-stained lips pressed to blood-stained forehead, the whispered words, "I love you," are almost too soft to be picked up by anyone but the dying girl. Her hands fall gently, and she comes to rest with a peaceful smile on her face, her eyes closed. She looks like an angel.

Advert for my Bedroom
By Ted Horton

Tamworth

Are you tired of going to bed in luxury? Do you want an escape into the realms of mediocre/poor guest hotels? Then come on down to Ted's Bedroom! You'll see ten tonnes of Warhammer figurines and Stephen King books crammed into 3 cubic metres of space!

It's warm and sometimes too warm as the boiler is in a cupboard in this room - it's the hottest room in the house! You'll have an aforementioned mediocre/poor sleep on my 1.5- star bed (drool patches and too many teddy bears included). Feast yourself upon my secret stash of pickled eggs, and watch constantly buffering YouTube videos on my prehistoric phone (please don't forget to dislike and unsubscribe my channel!).

I squeeze my spots by my mirror so the reflection you get back of yourself might not be the greatest or clearest. When you leave, be sure to pop a review in the box by my door (please note: the boxes contents are emptied onto a bonfire every Tuesday). What are you waiting for? Come and have a dismal* time at Ted's Bedroom!

*Please note that this advert is entirely fictional - my bedroom is awesome - and I have spent more time than ever in my house and room over the last year - and I love it! I'm just trying to be funny in this review!

Heavier Than Heaven, Lonelier Than God
By Iona Mandal

Edgbaston

While reading *Waiting for Godot*, I fell to sleep. It was a story of two characters engaged in conversation while waiting for Godot. Godot never arrives. I suppose in some ways, I am the man. Godot is death. My waiting room, the four walls of a casket. I am almost at the entrance of the cremator, waiting for my turn. 'I am of the earth and to the earth I shall return'. Every inch of skin, bone, cartilage, sweat, bile, reduced to ash. I am unable to leave my worldly possessions, I struggle for peaceful resolution to the other.

All my life, I have been waiting – for buses, interviews, phone calls, in supermarket queues and train stations. Now, I wait for my turn after death, behind others who died today. Death has no preference. In its hollow eyes, all lives equal, in conclusion. Rich, poor, young, old, none skip the queue. No VIP pass, no 'Priority' label. Just an orb of energy fleeting No Man's Land. The last sense one loses before death is hearing. In the indistinct muttering around, I sense frustration, sadness, exasperation, and contemplation.

I ponder over memories my mind handpicks to assess. Were my choices correct? Did my actions effect? I wonder. The Bible on my chest weighs me down; rosary coiled around my cold fingers. The doors of the incinerator edge open. A sudden warmth pounces; ruthless heat welcoming inside. My waiting comes to an end; what lies beyond, only rekindled. Another wait!

Grandma's House
By Lila Melnykevicova

Stoke-on-Trent

Last night something strange happened at grandma's house. It was the same old routine. She would open her door, greet us, give us a big sloppy kiss, we would wash our hands and then proceed to the dining room to eat the huge and filling roast dinner just as she would insist on having seconds and pile an even bigger portion onto your plate. Nothing extravagant about it, it was just a weekly visit to see grandma.

But you see, it's hard to explain, something was strange with grandma. Of course, she still did the same old routine, but it was more like she memorised the routine. She didn't actually do it. She had memorised her routine and all of the things she would say. It was almost as if grandma was scripted or auditioning for a lead part in a play. My parents acted normal; did they even notice grandma being stranger than usual? Of course not. They just ate the humongous roast dinner and made useless small talk.

But that's when I realised.

It wasn't grandma.

The Other Side
By Nusayba Nabeel

"Please don't let me fall, just don't let me fall!" I stood at the edge of the broken balcony. "I don't want to die!"

The raven-black wings on my back felt heavy and ungainly. After causing the death of my "friend", I had been cursed by her familiar as revenge, a powerfully magical dragon by the name of Abraxas. My hands trembled. I had never been a fan of heights.

"Look, I'm sorry! Please! Just get these stupid wings off me!" I begged, looking around in desperation and my eyes wide with fright. Nothing happened. I would have to jump to escape the building. I closed my eyes.

And jumped. My fears and doubts seemed to have been left on that balcony, and I felt confident and calm. As the wind rushed around me, making my eyes water, I heard the dragon's voice ringing. "You killed her. *You* did it. You don't deserve to be human anymore, because you have no humanity." He had summoned up all of his remaining magic to turn me into this… this *monster*. And then he had set himself and my apartment alight.

My wings spread open, and I soared. I felt free. My now-yellow eyes glowed in the darkness. I felt a strong magic course through me and realised that maybe this curse was a blessing in disguise. I chuckled. So maybe I did deserve to be a monster. But I was going to make sure I was the worst one of all.

Monsters next door

By Samarah Nadeem

I stayed with my neighbours for the afternoon yesterday, but little did I know that they were MONSTERS!

Suddenly, I realised that they looked exactly like my family, just opposite. I had a white t-shirt; the monster child had a black t-shirt.

When they handed out snacks, I was nearly sick, and that's not the worst bit that happened. They had blue octopus tentacles to eat and a brownish green coloured slime to drink. Between you and me, the slime looked a lot like toilet water mixed with snails; as we all know it's disgusting.

I went upstairs, to calm down and wash my mouth out, as I could still taste the horrible snacks in my mouth. I ran out screaming because their bathroom was covered in a sticky slime substance. I asked myself, ''Have they ever cleaned their bathroom?''

When I arrived back home, I locked all the doors and windows, just in case they were going to break down the front door. I did not leave the house for 2 days straight, until I realised that the monsters were not so bad. They were only trying to be nice, even though they look like big scary creatures just waiting to eat you when you go to sleep, the thought just scares me.

What would you do if you had a monster living next door?

The Scariest Monster Ever
By Samarah Nadeem

I am a terrifying monster, but my only weakness is a ladybird. Their bright red backs, with those black spots scare the life out of me.

Although I'm a scary monster, I can't scare little children, they're just not scared of me. I once tried, but they just stared and stared until they scared me.

No-one can ever see me because I'm very small. I can fit into the smallest places ever.

My favourite thing to do is scare other monsters, it's fun to watch them shiver. The best time to creep up on them is when they are sleeping because they won't see you coming up from behind.

I will scare every single person, dead or alive, providing that there aren't any ladybirds in my sight. If there are, I'll be the one screaming, ''Help me!''.

After all that I have just said, you'll think all I do is scare and terrify the souls of others, but I am very friendly when I want to be, ask any other monster and they'll agree with me.

I assure you that I'm still the scariest monster that you've ever seen.

All in a Day's Work
By Erin Oakley

"Now, what was it exactly I was looking for?" mumbled a man in an anachronistically puritanical top hat. "I needed something. A chair? A table perhaps? The curtains were—"

The sage floral footstool next to him in the aisle caught his eye; it would match his living room wallpaper. A large bottom, lurid in hot pink leggings, was positioned in front of the stool, blocking his way. The rest of the woman's body was not quite as large as her bottom alone and was almost entirely concealed. She was scouring the carpet for something, a coin perhaps, or her keys. There was barely room for a malnourished worm to squeeze its way past her, let alone a fifty-year-old man who refused to diet.

"Move thyself, Witch!" exclaimed Witchfinder Officer Flummery, brandishing his witch-finding cane (£50.99 from WitchfindersRus). "I seek to purchase that fine footstool that thou art obfuscating. Move and renounce Satan." Safe to say, Arthur Flummery, formerly a maths teacher, did not have much practical training as a witch-hunter. The most practice he did get was between the sales racks at budget clothing stores.

"What? Why do you look like you'm from the Tudor times or somat? Arthur?" The bottom, and the woman attached, slowly returned to an upright position. Now that he could see the woman's face, cold sweat dribbled down Arthur's spine.

It was his ex-wife, Marjory.

He turned tail and ran, all thoughts of furniture left with his witch-finding cane in the aisle.

Today
By Jenna O'Donnell

Leamington

Today is the day.

What an underwhelming phrase for a day I am certain will be entirely overwhelming. The weather is totally fitting too – it is a gloomy Monday, with a ghastly damp feeling clinging to the air, the type of sensation that makes your flesh crawl. Rain hammers angrily at my window, creating intricate patterns on the glass.

If it were any other day, I may have been inclined to perch on the window seat and recognise the beauty in the shapes on the glass, but today is different.

Today, the pounding of the rain feels as if it is not against the protective sheet of glass between myself and the outside world, but instead against my skull, harsh and jarring.

I have a mere five minutes to be fully clothed and out of my room, but I cannot seem to muster the energy to pull on my boots and climb to my feet. Instead, I allow myself to lay on my bedsheets, staring blankly at the patterns on my ceiling.

Will I ever return? Will I lay on this bed again? Will I come back to this life once I have left it?

I wonder.

I hope.

Mr Frizel The Man With Springs In His Feet
By Feranmi Ogunmiluyi

Bartley Green

Mr Frizel was visiting the zoo with his children. He jumped up very high because of the springs in his feet, meaning that he had a very good view of all the animals. His favourite were giraffes, as he had once jumped up onto one's head.

Anyway, Mr Frizel was having a first-class time when a man in a cloak as black as night appeared to him and hissed

"Find the watering can to jump even higher!"

"But how do I find it?" stuttered Mr Frizel.

"Penguinnnnn" were the man's last words.

Mr Frizel was very intrigued so he went to the penguin enclosure and saw a penguin playing the trumpet!

Mr Frizel jumped in, took the trumpet off the penguin then read the note that was on it. It said,

"Go to the tiger pit and play a tune then you will be able to jump to the Moon."

Immediately Mr Frizel went to the tiger pit and played a simple song on the trumpet. Slowly a watering can rose out of the ground and Mr Frizel took hold of it and jumped to the Moon.

He was never seen again.

Ashes
By Jasper Page

Kidderminster

The tree leaned in the wind, standing alone on the hill.
Standing alone in a sea of silence, a wilderness of
forgotten memories. The ashes of what was once my
home were still in the air. Still in the air after all those
years-returning to this spot was no small task. But the
tree growing on the ruins was slowly taking away the
memories, the dark times that none of us want to go
back to.

Childhood never ends for some and never was for
others. It never was for me. But seeing the ruins of my
old home, my old cottage, where I was born, it brings
me peace. I saw my parent's names carved into the
tree, slowly fading into the bark. Something that never
was, was returning. It felt good. Looking at my house,
its charred ruins, brought me at least a small amount of
comfort. I could never remember why I went there,
why I went back to the childhood that never was, what
was left of the house that burnt down.

The path leading from the cottage still had the same
pebbles, the same memories, and as I walked back
down the hill, I looked back once more at the great
Oak that had replaced my old home.

Cat Catastrophe
By Samuel Montgomery Parbutt

Ledbury

I jumped at Silvie and then realised she was like me, a survivor. I twitched my ears as if to say, "Have you been thrown out of a big blue door too?" and she waved her small white tail as if to say, "Yes, it was because I sat in my Protector's mouth and got it all hairy."

"Meow," I said, which means "I scratched mine on the arm."

"Oh well, let's go and find some food," Silvie said. So, we ventured into the garden. We collected carrots and lettuces and radishes before realising they were all disgusting.

We were still hungry, so we clawed up the wall onto the roof, and then up the chimney. We knocked off the grate and zipped down.

We landed with a thump at the bottom and sprang out of the fireplace and into the living room, leaving a trail of soot behind us. The mud erupted off us as we skidded around the corner and into the kitchen. We crawled up the table leg and devoured a tuna sandwich. Then we slept on the table with our tummies full of tuna.

When the Protector came back, he grabbed his slipper off his foot, so we scampered out of the house and into Silvie's to cause some trouble there. The big blue door slammed behind us.

My Storm
By Jeya Sandhar

Online Teen

Grey seeped into the pallid white fluff that sailed above, while specks of dust linked together - creating a dim, shadowy haze. Electricity crackled beyond them - ready to be unleashed from its slimy cage.

Averting my gaze from above, I focused on what was inside. The tower around me rapidly crumbled. Each brick scraping against another, like rusted parts of an ancient bike. Water recklessly washed the sides, eroding my only protection. Friends, family, happiness - all slowly melting under the weight of my troubles… under the weight of me.

Deadly spears rose from the water. They shifted towards me, blazing with hatred and disappointment. An orchestra swept the incessant waves, swept the electricity, and sang. Each note filled the flailing fortress. Waves rumbled, smashing against the mouldy stone as froth churned and spat out of the tide's mouth with Kraken-cruel intent.

There was nothing ahead of me but fear - no-one here to save me. Here in this world where I'm the conductor. Like starlight pulsing through the graphite abyss above, lightning came in shards. Ferocious wind whipped my hair as I was hastily thrown against the cold concrete. A familiar iciness trickled in. It reached for me, penetrating my conscience. I felt a sharp, glacial mist filling my mind, jumbling my thoughts, steadily worrying me. Memories flashed violently in front of me, flicking past faster than I could comprehend.

But I still felt them, they were leaving me... was this why I was stuck there?

Was it all my fault?

Trade
By Emily Shields

Rugby

I noticed a pulsing light in my sister's room and when I walked in, I heard a tinkling ice-cream-van noise; the room was minimal and there was nothing to suggest where the sound, or the light, was coming from. I continued to my room, putting the experience aside as a dream.

The minute I entered my room, I regretted my decision: the screen on my laptop read, pure as day, "I'm coming. Watch your back." I ran. My face was as white as snow and my heart felt like a butterfly, I could see the open front door before me as I ran, my arms outstretched as if to catch a moving train, but then "Bang". It shut tantalisingly close, sending me skidding into it.

A whispering sound and misty wall surrounded my coming closer and closer, catching me like a net: "You're ours now, it seemed to say" as it suffocated me. From the cloud, a murky, white, figure extricated itself floating towards me its arms outstretched. As its arm touched mine, the world went black.

I awoke in a white room. Another milky apparition approached me "An eye for an eye, a tooth for a tooth… a life for a life," they whispered the words trickling into my ears like snake venom, "Say goodbye.". A screen in front of me flickered on, showing my family. Tears trickling down my face, I closed my eyes and murmured, "goodbye…" as I descended into darkness, "goodbye…".

The Joys of Summer
By Avani Singh

Online Junior

As the wholesome aroma of summer packs the air; the joy, which was once in a deep winter slumber, is revived!

Quaint blossoms and flowers bloom, providing food for a myriad of insects. The gleaming sun shines its glamorous rays. Mellifluous and melodious birds tweet sweetly like an angel's voice. As the fresh summer odour wafts up your nose, all your worries are washed away. The meadows of fruits are filled with succulent berries alongside beautiful butterflies and lovely ladybirds.

Beaches are lively, merry and jolly. The ice cream van plays its flamboyant tune incessantly while the repetitive bounce of beach balls echoes all around.

These endless sounds and views are what makes summer special and many people's favourite season!

In The Alley
By Amelie Stewart

Ledbury

It was dark and dusty in the alleyway. To be quite honest, I'm not quite sure how or why I ended up here but hopefully it will cure my boredom. Mother always told me if life gives me something then I should take it.

For context, I get lost a lot and this happens to be one of those times (unfortunately). I looked up and saw the glimmering sun through the dark misty clouds. The contrast made me wonder if I'd ever see sunlight again, unless I got myself out of this situation...

Before I could even blink, I fell for what felt like hours. I couldn't move. I was trapped. I couldn't breathe at all. My head was spinning, my heart was pounding, and I was struggling to breathe. I saw pure blackness surrounding me, but I couldn't reach out to it. It was too far. I tried to get up, I tried everything, but my body fell again and again.

And then it hit me. Or maybe it didn't. Maybe this is all a nightmare. I lay and hoped my prediction wasn't correct. All the memories came rushing back, as if I had just woken up. I turned around to see the alleyway

again. I could tell it was certainly not a dream.
Nothing seems real now. At least, I don't think it is…

Miscellaneous

These pieces written as diary entries, letters and scripts were written during or inspired by Spark Young Writers group sessions.

20th May 2018
By Ben Haycock

Leamington

It may please you to know that I still hate you. You mean as much to me as the fierce gale and painful sleet that seems to have started here in the Big Apple.

I head south for the exotic wilderness of Havana tomorrow in the spectre of a 1588 galleon you and I tore through and robbed blind a couple of years back. I leave behind the old shack of pretty little crimes and mass murder we used to call work: did I say we? I meant I.

Me and a noble crew of fine grave robbers I found lying about in the streets are to make our journey via ghost ship. Tonight, we dine on steak and chips, knowing it might be our last meal in the grimy city of New York. It pains me to say that I miss working with you. Your little schemes and annoying intelligence may be the only reason I am able to make this journey.

Anyway, I ought to head off: this storm's getting fiercer by the minute. I'll avoid sending you a postcard upon my arrival.

Goodbye, Sam.

My Giant Praying Mantis
By Evie Hodgetts

Worcester

Dear Diary,

Hello! My name's Ben, and I'm fascinated by animals. When I'm older, I'm going to have a house full of animals. We have to hope they don't eat each other, though! Actually, that might really be a problem. I'll figure that out later, though.

A few weeks ago, I got a giant praying mantis. He's ginormous, and I named him Elijah. He eats a lot, usually crickets and manky dead mice from a special section of the pet shop, but I sometimes try to catch insects from the garden for him too, although his all-time favourite thing to eat is chocolate hobnobs. They're my favourite too, which is funny, isn't it? We often steal packets from the kitchen and eat them in secret. If mum found out, she'd be cross, because we eat them a lot and might get fat. We have to be careful not to leave crumbs, like the breadcrumb trail in Hansel and Gretel. It might lead her to us snacking on them under the covers!

I am taking him to school tomorrow for Show and Tell, and we're both so excited! My teacher said I could bring him in. We're going to be the best in the whole class!

I should probably go to sleep now. We have a big day tomorrow!
Love Ben xxx

Dear diary,

I didn't know he liked long blonde hair so much. I think I'm in trouble.

Ben xxx

The Letters
By Alessia Stokoe

Online Teen

Dear Mother, Father and Lucille,

I no longer believe any of these letters are reaching you, let alone that I will receive a reply. I miss you, more than you could ever understand.

It seems to me that I have been suffering the same bleak skies and frigid storms for years. Perhaps it really is the same day, stretching on forever like the barbed wire around me. I have lost track of everything. The men who fight alongside me are strangers, dying before I can learn their names. Their faces are nothing but a smudge against my mind.

I am broken now, I know it. I can feel my soul sticking out at twisted angles like a broken limb. All I can hope for is numbness and an end.

Vincent

Lucille raised a hand to her cheeks, expecting them to be damp with tears, but they were completely dry. It had been over a month since the family had received a letter informing them of Vincent's death. Lucille's parents were grief-stricken, so why wasn't she? Shouldn't she be mourning too?

She knew she couldn't. Not until she dug up the truth about these *letters*. After Vincent had died, one would appear in his drawer every few days. Each letter was written in his handwriting and had that day's date in the corner. Lucille didn't know who was delivering them, or how, but what she did know was that could only mean one thing.

Vincent was alive. But for how long?

Invictus
By Abel Neto

Edgbaston

EXT. CAPITAL RUINS - TIME UNKNOWN

Misty, lightly obscured setting. Lots of debris lays on the ground. Weather-beaten ruins scatter the setting. INVICTUS- robed darkly, glimpsed treading through the fog.

NARRATOR
To the miners, he was but a legend. A myth invented by man to entertain their playful minds.
[Fog thickens.]

INVICTUS is seen standing rigidly, hood tilted downwards. He appears to be looking at something on the floor.

NARRATOR
All myths have an origin- fantasy or not.

INVICTUS slowly tilts his head back up.

NARRATOR
But this one - it's real.

Scarcely visible clouds cluster together, turning the pale sky a morbid black. INVICTUS is nowhere to be seen.

NARRATOR
It burrows into your mind. It shrouds itself with your doubt, only to dissipate before your very mind.

A mighty fork of lightning erupts from the very folds of the sky. It briefly illuminates the ruins, exposing its torn silhouette and just perhaps, just perhaps, a moving shadow.

NARRATOR
(Talking faster, with a hint of mania)
It's here. I've seen it. Its aura has long ago overridden me. I am not mad; I only strive to discover the undiscovered. I am -

NARRATOR is interrupted, as the figure of a creature slowly strides towards the NARRATOR. The NARRATOR - a small man, eyes bloodshot and wide with lunacy - is seen hunched behind a pillar, writing in a book. INVICTUS approaches him, pulling his hood up.

NARRATOR screams.

Spark
Young Writers

Creative writing groups for children and young people in the West Midlands

£90 per year
£9 per session
Aged 8–17

writingwestmidlands.org

Printed in Great Britain
by Amazon

67086072R00061